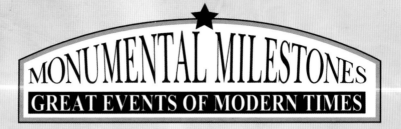

MONUMENTAL MILESTONES
GREAT EVENTS OF MODERN TIMES

The Story of
the Holocaust

Children imprisoned at the Auschwitz concentration camp await rescue in 1945.

Mitchell Lane
PUBLISHERS

P.O. Box 196
Hockessin, Delaware 19707

Titles in the Series

The Dawn of Aviation:
The Story of the Wright Brothers

The Story of the Attack on Pearl Harbor

Breaking the Sound Barrier:
The Story of Chuck Yeager

Top Secret: The Story of the
Manhattan Project

The Story of the Holocaust

The Civil Rights Movement

Exploring the North Pole:
The Story of Robert Edwin
Peary and Matthew Henson

The Story of the Great Depression

The Cuban Missile Crisis:
The Cold War Goes Hot

The Fall of the Berlin Wall

Disaster in the Indian Ocean:
Tsunami 2004

MONUMENTAL MILESTONES
GREAT EVENTS OF MODERN TIMES

The Story of the Holocaust

Children imprisoned at the Auschwitz concentration camp await rescue in 1945.

2006

Jim Whiting

Printing   1   2   3   4   5   6   7   8   9

Library of Congress Cataloging-in-Publication Data
    Whiting, Jim, 1943–
        The story of the Holocaust / by Jim Whiting
                p. cm. — (Monumental milestones)
        Includes bibliographical references and index.
        ISBN 1-58415-400-4 (library bound)
    1. Holocaust, Jewish (1939-1945)—Juvenile literature. I. Title. II. Series.
D804.34.W52 2005
940.53'18—dc22   2005004247

ABOUT THE AUTHOR: Jim Whiting has been a remarkably versatile and accomplished journalist, writer, editor, and photographer for more than 30 years. A voracious reader since early childhood, Mr. Whiting has written and edited about 200 nonfiction children's books. His subjects range from authors to zoologists and include contemporary pop icons and classical musicians, saints and scientists, emperors and explorers. Representative titles include *The Life and Times of Franz Liszt*, *The Life and Times of Julius Caesar*, *Charles Schulz*, and *Juan Ponce de Leon*.

Other career highlights are a lengthy stint publishing *Northwest Runner*, the first piece of original fiction to appear in *Runners World* magazine, hundreds of descriptions and venue photographs for America Online, e-commerce product writing, sports editor for the *Bainbridge Island Review*, light verse in a number of magazines, and acting as the official photographer for the Antarctica Marathon.

He lives in Washington state with his wife and two teenage sons.

PHOTO CREDITS: Cover, pp. 1, 3, 6, 12—Robert Hunt Library; p. 14—Corbis; pp. 18, 24, 26, 27, 30—Robert Hunt Library; p. 33—Andrea Pickens; p. 38 Robert Hunt Library

PUBLISHER'S NOTE: This story contains graphic information regarding the Holocaust. In the hopes that it will never happen again, the publisher believes young adults and children need to read about the horrors of the Holocaust.

This story is based on the author's extensive research, which he believes to be accurate. Documentation of such research is contained on page 46.

The internet sites referenced herein were active as of the publication date. Due to the fleeting nature of some websites, we cannot guarantee they will all be active when you are reading this book.

Contents

The Story of the Holocaust

Jim Whiting

Chapter 1 Liberation 7

              FYInfo*: *The Diary of Anne Frank* 11

Chapter 2 The Nazis Take Over 13

              FYInfo: The 1936 Summer Olympics 23

Chapter 3 *Einsatzgruppen* 25

              FYInfo: The Warsaw Ghetto Uprising 29

Chapter 4 The Final Solution 31

              FYInfo: The Plot to Kill Hitler 37

Chapter 5 Justice 39

              FYInfo: The Nuremberg Trials 42

Chronology 43

Timeline in History 44

Chapter Notes 45

Further Reading 46

           For Young Adults 46

           Works Consulted 46

           On the Internet 46

Glossary 47

Pronunciation Guide 47

Index 48

*For Your Information

At the Bergen-Belsen concentration camp, British troops discovered approximately 10,000 unburied corpses.

The soldiers liberated the camp in April 1945. Unlike the situation in many other concentration camps, prisoners at Bergen-Belsen were not gassed. Rather, they were starved to death. In desperation, some prisoners turned to cannibalism.

Liberation

On the morning of April 29, 1945, Sergeant Joe Sacco and his buddies in the 92nd Signal Battalion had reason to feel optimistic. They had been in action for more than nine months, and they knew that World War II in Europe was almost over. They were the lucky ones. They had survived. Now they had one more task. They had been assigned to help a group of infantrymen liberate a prison near the town of Dachau (DAH-cow), in southern Germany.

As they drew closer to their objective, they could see and hear the firing from American soldiers who had already taken positions near the high brick walls topped with rolls of razor-sharp barbed wire. The fighting didn't last long. When it was over, Sacco and the other men approached the gate of the camp. They became aware of a particularly bad smell. They made crude jokes about what might have caused it.

Moments later they stepped inside the front gate. They saw what was causing the smell. There were no more jokes. Many years later, Sacco had no difficulty remembering the horrifying scene.

"I saw the dead—women, children, old men, babies—beaten, starved, stabbed, shot, butchered, and left to rot on the ground," he said. "Most were wearing the tattered striped uniform of a prisoner. Others were completely naked. Some were so emaciated that I couldn't tell if they were male or female."[1]

This was their introduction to the German concentration camp at Dachau. It seemed that they couldn't take more than a few steps that morning without encountering fresh horrors. They saw a shooting

gallery. Many of the targets had been youngsters. The youngsters had tried to sprint across a stage as German soldiers with high-powered rifles shot at them. The pile of corpses at the far end showed that few of the Germans had missed their mark.

Shaken, the soldiers walked over to a nearby railroad siding. Box-cars and cattle cars were packed with dozens of corpses. The victims had starved to death. Inside one of the cars was a young woman holding her infant to her breast. Both were dead.

Upset that he hadn't arrived in time to save these people, Sacco began crying. He wasn't alone. Men who had witnessed the horrors of combat for months broke down at the sight of so many bodies. A few minutes later, they went farther inside the camp. Thousands of scrawny prisoners were pressing against the fence. Many were Jews. Others were communists, Gypsies, homosexuals, even Jehovah's Witnesses. Their only "crime" was being different from "normal" Germans.

Almost all were literally walking skeletons. A loss of 50 or 60 percent body weight was common. Up to 1,600 prisoners had been crammed into individual barracks that had been designed to accommodate just over 200. They had existed with almost no food. When they heard the shooting a few minutes earlier, they had been afraid that the guards were about to murder them. Now they realized that their ordeal was over. They would live. Most of them, that is. Some were so near death that they died within a few hours or days of the rescue. Others, given decent food for the first time in months or even years, couldn't hold it down. It was too much for their fragile systems. They too died.

Nearby, a group of captured German guards were lined up against a wall. They laughed among themselves and shouted insults at the American soldiers. One GI snapped. He picked up a machine gun and mowed down some of the Germans before an officer could stop him.

The healthier prisoners began a grim task. They stacked the bodies on top of open wagons. Then they dragged the wagons to a single-story building. It was the crematorium. To avoid the outbreak of disease,

it was necessary to burn the bodies of the dead prisoners as quickly as possible. A thick cloud of smoke billowed out of the tall smokestack.

Sacco and the others walked over to a building that appeared to be an infirmary. It wasn't. An infirmary is a place where people go to get well. German doctors had used this facility to make people get worse. They tortured prisoners in medical "experiments." Sometimes they injected them with diseases to study their reactions. Or they would put the arms or legs of prisoners in vises. Then they would turn the handles. Careful records indicated how much force was necessary to crush the bones.

Close by was a real infirmary. Modern and well maintained, it was for the use of German army personnel. Angry GIs forced the patients out and used the facility to begin the heartbreaking task of caring for the seriously ill prisoners.

Also on the compound was a kennel with dozens of vicious dogs. They had been trained to track down the few people who had managed to escape and maul them. Sometimes the guards had opened the doors and let them attack prisoners for no reason.

The next morning, the soldiers went to the town of Dachau. They rounded up the German residents and forced them to walk through the prison. Many of the residents gasped in disbelief—or at least they appeared to. No one could tell how much the townspeople actually knew about what had been going on so close to their homes.

General Dwight D. Eisenhower, the commander of Allied forces in Europe, ordered as many American soldiers as possible to visit Dachau. As Joe Sacco concluded, "Each of us finally and forever understood why destiny had called us to travel so far from the land of our birth and fight for people we did not know. And so it was here, in this place abandoned by God and accursed by men, that we came to discover the meaning of our mission."[2]

Dachau, which began operations on March 22, 1933, was the first concentration camp that German dictator Adolf Hitler established. The term *concentration camp* comes from the fact that many

"undesirables" were "concentrated" in a small area. This concentration made it much easier to control them, usually with a small number of guards. No one knows how many people lost their lives at Dachau. Officially, the number is about 30,000. Others say 50,000. Some estimates run as high as nearly 240,000.

Dachau was just one of the concentration camps that were built at Hitler's orders. Their names are engraved on human consciousness. The roster includes Belzec, Bergen-Belsen, Buchenwald, Chelmno, Majdanek, Maly Trostenets, Mauthausen, Ravensbrück, Sachsenhausen, Sobibór, and Treblinka (see page 47 for pronunciations).

And above all, Auschwitz.

In January 2005, leaders from many world nations gathered at this small village in Poland. So did some of the former inmates who had managed to survive the horrors of a system that was designed to keep them from surviving. They were remembering the sixtieth anniversary of its liberation by the Red Army—soldiers of the Soviet Union—as it swept toward Berlin, the capital of Germany.

As with the dead at Dachau, no one knows how many people perished in the gas chambers at Auschwitz. The lowest estimate is 1.5 million, nearly all of whom were Jews. Many more Jews were gassed at the other camps. Others died from shooting, hanging, starvation, and disease. In all, an estimated 6 million Jews were murdered. They were victims of Hitler's desire for Germany and the other parts of Europe he controlled to be *Judenfrei*—free of Jews.

When Adolf Hitler came to power, he proclaimed that he was establishing an empire that would endure for a thousand years. Fortunately, he was wrong. His cruel regime lasted for just over twelve years. He gave it the name the Third Reich.

History has given this twelve-year period of mass slaughter a very different name: the Holocaust. The original meaning of *Holocaust* was "sacrifice by fire." The horrors that Adolf Hitler unleashed gave it an entirely new definition: "complete destruction of an entire group of people." Only the military defeat of Germany kept Hitler from carrying out his murderous intention.

Anne Frank

Probably the most famous Holocaust victim was a teenaged German Jewish girl named Anne Frank. Soon after Hitler came to power, Anne's parents, Otto and Edith Frank, recognized the danger he posed. They moved to Amsterdam, The Netherlands. Their apparent safety came to an end in May 1940 when the German army swept through the country. For two years, the family lived under conditions that grew increasingly threatening.

Anne was given a diary as a present for her thirteenth birthday. By that time, the deportation of Jews to Auschwitz had begun. Less than a month later, the Franks went into hiding above Otto's place of business. Trusted employees provided them with food. Eventually four other people joined the Franks: Hermann and Auguste van Pels, their sixteen-year-old son Peter, and Fritz Pfeffer, a family friend.

Anne's diary faithfully records her life for more than two years. At first, she intended it solely for her own use. Then she heard a radio broadcast urging people living under Nazi tyranny to keep a record of their experiences. Anne decided she would publish her diary when the war was over.

Her final entry is dated August 1, 1944. Three days later, the small group was arrested. They were sent to Auschwitz and immediately split up. Anne and her sister were transferred to Bergen-Belsen, where they died from typhus in the winter of 1945. Her father was the only one of the eight to survive.

Fortunately, Anne's diary also survived. In 1947, Otto decided to honor his daughter's wish and publish it. Since then, it has been translated into more than 60 languages. Countless millions of readers have been moved by its description of Anne's attempt to live a human life in the midst of inhuman circumstances.

Part of the final entry reads, "I have a reputation for being boy-crazy as well as a flirt, a smart aleck and a reader of romances."[3] Over the years, she has acquired a much different reputation. *Time* magazine named her one of the 100 most important people of the twentieth century.

Adolf Hitler was a man of str deadly—convictions.

No one knows why Hitler hated Jewish people so much. It is just as mysterious why so many German soldiers and civilians went along with his grisly program. One possible reason is that there was a long tradition of strong anti-Jewish feelings in Europe.

The Nazis Take Over

For good reason, nearly everyone today associates Adolf Hitler with the Holocaust and the crimes against the Jews. But anti-Semitism, the hatred of Jews, has roots that go back nearly two millennia.

Following their unsuccessful revolt against Roman authority in A.D. 67, the Jews were forced to leave the Holy Land, even though it had been their homeland for more than a thousand years. Most settled in Europe. When Christianity became the dominant religion in the Roman Empire a few centuries later, Christians tried to convert Jews to the "true religion." They were hardly ever successful. Even so, the two religious groups lived in peace for several hundred years.

In the eleventh century—during the Middle Ages—conditions changed. Jews began to be forced to live apart from Christians in many cities. They were confined to relatively small areas known as ghettos. The intention was to reduce contact between members of the two religions as much as possible. Because Christians were forbidden by the church to lend money and charge interest, that task fell to Jews. Many Christians fell into debt. They hated the Jews to whom they owed money, and they blamed them for their financial circumstances. It also became a common belief among Christians that Jews were responsible for the crucifixion of Jesus. They believed that Jews kidnapped Christian children, murdered them, and used their blood for secret rituals. They blamed Jews for spreading diseases such as the Black Death. Crusaders on their way to liberate the Holy Land from Muslim infidels often slaughtered entire Jewish populations that they encountered on their way.

Some of these beliefs existed at the highest levels of Christianity. In 1492, King Ferdinand and Queen Isabella of Spain financed Christopher Columbus's expedition that resulted in the European discovery of the New World. At the same time, they were expelling all Jews from Spain unless they converted to Christianity. Martin Luther's horror at the excesses of the Catholic Church led to the Protestant Reformation in the early years of the sixteenth century. Luther, however, was also violently anti-Semitic. In a 1543 pamphlet called *The Jews and Their Lies*, he described Jews as "poisonous bitter worms."[1] Equating them with the devil, he advocated several methods of dealing with them: destroying their homes, capturing and confining them, expelling them from

King Ferdinand of Spain

Born in 1452, Ferdinand married his cousin Isabella when he was seventeen and she was eighteen. They ruled Spain together for several decades.

Germany. Four centuries later, Hitler took all these "recommendations" to heart.

The majority of Jews eventually settled in Eastern Europe. Life there could still be dangerous. In nineteenth- and early twentieth-century Russia, Jews were subjected to government-sponsored riots called pogroms. Many Jews, including "God Bless America" composer Irving Berlin, fled to the safety of the United States and other countries.

Conditions for Jews in Western Europe had improved a great deal since the Middle Ages. There were no more massacres. Restrictions against them had eased. Some married Christians. In Germany, despite the legacy of Martin Luther, many Jewish people became important members of German society. They served as doctors, lawyers, scientists, and artists.

Throughout Europe, prejudice against Jews was never far below the surface. German political writer Wilhelm Marr invented the term *anti-Semitism* in 1873. Before that time, Jews had been disliked because of what they believed. Now they were disliked because they were seen as a separate race of people, rather than just people who practiced a different religion.

In 1894, a Jewish French army officer named Alfred Dreyfus was accused of being a spy and sentenced to life imprisonment at the notorious Devil's Island. The "evidence" soon proved to be false. Many people believed that he was convicted because of his religion. The case rocked France—and much of Europe—for several years. In 1905 a document called *The Protocols of the Elders of Zion,* the secret plan for world domination by the "international Jewish conspiracy," was published in Russia. Even though it was later proved to be a forgery put together by Russian secret police and was false in every respect, at the time it was widely believed to be true. Many people, especially in the Middle East, still accept it as genuine.

World War I, which began in 1914, proved to be a disaster both for Germany and for the many Jews who fought on both sides. It was bad

enough that millions of young men—thousands of whom were Jewish— perished in more than four years of combat.

Even worse were the political consequences. In Russia, postwar pogroms resulted in the deaths of tens of thousands of Jews. When Germany surrendered in November 1918, many Germans couldn't understand why their government had given up. Germany was proud of its military tradition. The country hadn't been a battlefield. All the fighting had taken place on foreign soil. It didn't take long for a belief to begin circulating that Germany hadn't actually lost the war. It had been "stabbed in the back." The main candidates for this misleading charge of treason were communists and Jews.

Led by Great Britain and France, the victors forced the Germans to sign the Treaty of Versailles. The treaty humiliated Germany and imposed harsh terms. The country had to give up some of its territory. Its armed forces had to be drastically reduced. It had to accept responsibility for starting the war and pay massive reparations. These conditions led to desperate economic conditions. In the early 1920s, the country suffered a period of massive inflation. Many people lost their life savings. When that situation improved, the Great Depression in the United States soon spread to much of the rest of world. Germany fell into an economic depression of its own.

The nation's citizens looked to Adolf Hitler to solve their economic problems and restore their status as an important nation.

Hitler was born in Braunau am Inn, Austria, on April 20, 1889. At the age of eighteen, with both of his parents dead, the young man moved to Vienna to pursue his ambition of becoming an artist. He wanted to attend art school, but his applications were rejected twice. He lived a meager existence for several years, selling postcards and some of his paintings.

By this time he had acquired the beliefs that he would eventually put to murderous effect: anti-Semitism and the superiority of the Aryan race—the German and Nordic *Volk* (people). He believed that Jews—as

well as the Slavic peoples who lived in Russia and most of Eastern Europe—were not only the natural enemies of Germans but also inferior to them. They were *Untermenschen* (subhuman). The blond and blue-eyed Aryans, on the other hand, were *Herrenrasse*—the "master race."

Hitler enlisted in the German army when World War I broke out and served with distinction. He earned the coveted Iron Cross for bravery and rose to the rank of corporal. When the war was over, he joined the German Workers' Party. It was one of the numerous right-wing political groups that sprang up in the chaotic political conditions that characterized immediate postwar Germany. The group was small, and he soon became one of its most important members. He changed its name to the National Socialist German Workers' Party. The shorter version of its name would become infamous. It was *Nazi*.

Soon the failed artist discovered his true talent. He was one of the twentieth century's most mesmerizing public speakers. He used this talent to gain leadership of the party in late 1921. He also adopted its most famous symbol: the swastika. While today we consider it a symbol of racial hatred and intolerance, the swastika actually has a three-thousand-year history of standing for life and good luck.

Hitler found two targets for his oratory: the harsh Versailles Treaty and "the Jews." His speeches added thousands of members to the party's rolls. These numbers emboldened him to take action. On the evening of November 8, 1923, he led hundreds of Nazis to break up a meeting led by Bavarian state commissioner Gustav Ritter von Kahr. Hitler "arrested" Kahr and proclaimed that a national revolution was under way. The incident became known as the Beer Hall Putsch because it took place at one of Munich's massive drinking establishments.

The "revolution" flopped. Local police quickly arrested Hitler, and he was sentenced to five years in prison. Far from branding him as a failure, the incident catapulted Hitler to prominence. He spent a comfortable nine months in prison being treated as a celebrity and dictating his autobiography, *Mein Kampf* (My Struggle). As a book, it is terrible,

Hermann Göring was Adolf Hitler's most trusted henchman.

Göring served as a fighter pilot during World War I. He was among the first men to join Adolf Hitler after the war. He held several important positions in Hitler's government. The most important was commanding the Luftwaffe, the German Air Force.

poorly written. It is also terrible in another way—in terms of its description of what was to come.

The Nazi Party continued to grow, helped along by Hitler's promise to improve the hard times that most Germans were going through. Just as important were the annual Nazi Party rallies that Hitler staged in the city of Nuremberg. Historian Gerhard Rempel observes that these rallies, which featured tens of thousands of people packed closely together, were "masterpieces of theatrical art, with the most carefully devised effects. . . . To see the films of the Nuremberg rallies even today is to be recaptured by the hypnotic effect of thousands of men marching in perfect order, the music of the massed bands, the forest of standards and flags, the vast perspectives of the stadium, the smoking torches, the dome of searchlights. The sense of power, of force and unity was irresistible,

and all converged with a mounting crescendo of excitement on the supreme moment when the Führer himself made his entry."[2]

By 1932 the party was the largest in the Reichstag, the German parliament. Early in 1933, the popular German president, Paul von Hindenburg, summoned Hitler and made him the chancellor. The one-time corporal now headed the government.

Hitler's meteoric rise wasn't due entirely to his own efforts. His second-in-command in the Nazi Party was Hermann Göring, who had been a pilot during World War I. Göring established a political police force called the *Geheime Staatspolizei.* Shortened to *Gestapo,* it was a name that would spread terror for more than a decade.

Another important Nazi was Heinrich Himmler. Kind-looking in glasses that made him look like a mild-mannered accountant, Himmler would soon be in charge of carrying out the increasingly harsh decrees against the Jews. He used another organization to achieve his goals. This was the *Schutzstaffel,* or "defense echelon." Abbreviated to SS, it would inspire the same terror throughout Europe as the Gestapo.

A third was Ernst Röhm, who headed the *Sturmabteilung* (storm detachment), or SA. Röhm and his men had been among Hitler's earliest and most enthusiastic supporters. Many were little better than thugs and street fighters, whose aggressive tactics had often been used in the party's formative years to intimidate opponents.

One of Hitler's first acts as chancellor was pushing through the Enabling Law. It gave him the power to create laws without bothering to have the Reichstag vote on them. Two weeks later he virtually eliminated the power of the many smaller states that had become united in 1871 to form modern-day Germany. Soon he stripped away the power of any other individuals or groups that might oppose him.

He needed someplace to keep his opponents. He established Dachau in March and quickly sent thousands of political prisoners there. Many more would follow.

In April, Hitler urged a one-day boycott against Jewish businesses. There was almost no violence. Restrictive laws against Jews began pouring out of the Reichstag.

Six months later, Hitler announced that Germany was withdrawing from the League of Nations, the precursor to the United Nations. Symbolically, Germany was repudiating the Versailles Treaty.

Hitler still had one source of uneasiness: Ernst Röhm and his 2.5 million SA members. Even though Röhm was one of his best friends, Hitler was afraid that he wanted to overthrow him. On the night of June 30, 1934, Hitler took action. Several members of Himmler's SS dragged Röhm out of bed. By the following morning, he was dead. So were scores of other SA leaders. The incident became known as the Night of the Long Knives. When Hindenburg died just over a month later, Hitler assumed supreme power and gave himself the title Der Führer (The Leader). Soon he proclaimed the Thousand-Year Reich.

Two laws passed at Nuremberg in 1935 put further restrictions on Jews. The State Citizenship Law stripped Jews of their German citizenship, while the Law for the Protection of German Blood and German Honor forbade Jews from marrying German citizens. It also said that a person with one or more Jewish grandparents was considered a Jew. Many Germans who fell into this category were practicing Christians. It didn't matter—they were now considered Jews.

To create neighborhoods that were *Judenfrei,* many Jews were uprooted from villages and small towns and resettled in larger cities. This was the first "solution" to what soon became known as the "Jewish question."

The second solution quickly followed. Jews were encouraged to leave the country entirely. Many took advantage of the "opportunity," even though in many cases it meant leaving homes that they had lived in for generations. In the succeeding months and years, they also had to leave behind increasingly large amounts of their personal property and wealth.

Soon Hitler began directing his energy toward the expansion of German territory, a concept that became known as *lebensraum* (living room, or living space). The first target was the Rhineland, a region bordering France, Belgium, and the Netherlands that Germany had been forced to give up after World War I. Against the advice of his generals, Hitler sent troops of the newly enlarged German army into the Rhineland in March 1936, even though it was a clear violation of the Versailles Treaty. Most historians believe this would have been the best chance to halt Hitler in his tracks and prevent the bloodshed that followed. Yet France and Great Britain did nothing. Two years later German soldiers marched into Austria. Many Austrians welcomed them. In what was known as the *Anschluss* (Annexation), Austria became a part of Germany. That fall, after coming to an agreement with Great Britain and France, Hitler took over part of Czechoslovakia. He assured their leaders that he had no further intentions to add territory to Germany. British Prime Minister Neville Chamberlain, who believed in avoiding war by appeasement, announced that he had secured "peace in our time." He couldn't have been more wrong.

In October 1938, thousands of Jews who were originally from Poland and had established homes in Germany were loaded onto railroad cars and taken across the Polish border. At first the Polish government refused to take them. For several weeks they lived in horse stables. Finally the Poles accepted them. A young man named Herschel Grynszpan, a student in Paris, was upset because his parents were included in this deportation. He entered the German embassy in Paris and shot to death a minor official stationed there. The Nazis reacted by staging a massive riot against the Jews. On the night of November 9, 1938, rioters threw bricks and stones into windows of Jewish stores and synagogues. Many ran inside and threw the contents out onto the streets. Nearly a hundred Jews were murdered, and countless others were beaten by the rampaging mobs. Many were sent to concentration camps. The

incident became known as *Kristallnacht,* or the Night of the Broken Glass. It was a grim foretaste of what was to come.

By this point, many Jews had left Germany. Among them were noted scientists, such as Albert Einstein, who would eventually use their knowledge against their homeland and help defeat Hitler.

Those who hadn't left yet faced another problem. Jews who wished to emigrate had to have someplace to go. Many wanted to go to Palestine. The Arabs who lived there were angry at the growing numbers of Jews in the land. The British, who controlled Palestine, made it virtually impossible for any more Jews to enter. Increasingly anxious Jews also found that many countries weren't admitting them. The United States, for example, had rigid immigration quotas for different groups of people. Once those quotas were met, no more could come.

In 1938 the British made one exception, allowing an unspecified number of certain children to enter the country. Between 1938 and 1940, about 10,000 children entered Britain through the Kindertransport (Children's Transport) program. The older ones bid tearful goodbyes to their parents, thinking that they would never see them again. Almost always they were right.

German dictator Adolf Hitler wanted to use the 1936 Olympic Games in Berlin to showcase the racial superiority of the German people and the improvements in the German way of life that had taken place under his regime. Because he had already demonstrated his extreme prejudice against Jews, a number of people in the United States wanted to stay away from the Olympics to show their disapproval of his actions. In a narrow vote, the U.S. Olympic Committee voted to participate in the Games.

Hitler knew how to put on a good show. Among many spectacular touches, Games organizers inaugurated the now-familiar torch relay. A torch was kindled by the sun at the site of the ancient Olympics in Olympia, Greece, then carried

Jesse Owens

to Berlin by a succession of hundreds of runners. "No previous games had seen such a spectacular organization nor such a lavish display of entertainment," wrote journalist and historian William Shirer. "The visitors, especially those from England and America, were greatly impressed by what they saw; apparently a happy, healthy, friendly people united under Hitler."[3] One reason for this seeming harmony was that the Nazis had removed signs such as *Juden unerwuenscht* (Jews not welcome) just before the influx of foreign visitors.

Germany won more medals than any other country. But Jesse Owens, an African-American athlete, won four gold medals—100 meters, 200 meters, 4x100 meters relay, and long jump—in a blow to Hitler's claim of his country's racial superiority. German newspapers insultingly referred to Owens and other African Americans as "auxiliaries."

There was a German hero at these Games, though not in the way that Hitler had intended. In the preliminaries of the long jump, Owens fouled on his first two tries. If it happened again, he would be out of the competition. At that point, Luz Long, a German who was his chief competitor, came up to him and suggested that he change his takeoff point. Owens followed the suggestion and easily qualified. Long's generous gesture cost him a gold medal, for he finished second to Owens. Sadly, he was killed in combat during the war.

A group of brownshirts parades
German town in support of Adol

Officially known as the
Sturmabteilung, ("storm
detachment," or SA for
short), these men were
called brownshirts because
of the distinctive color of
their uniform. Many were
little more than thugs. They
enjoyed beating up Hitler's
opponents. Hitler also used
them to attack Jewish
businesses.

Einsatzgruppen

Just as no one knows all the reasons why Hitler hated Jews so much, no one knows when Hitler gave the order to begin killing them.

The road to the start of World War II is clearer. On September 1, 1939, Hitler invaded Poland. His army quickly swept over the country. In the space of a few weeks, Hitler had added three million Jews to the populations he controlled. There were far too many to handle using his first two solutions.

The next "solution" was an echo of the Middle Ages. Jews were forced into tiny, tightly packed ghettos. There was little food. Diseases were rampant. In large cities such as Warsaw and Lodz, hundreds died every week. But for Hitler, the Jews weren't dying fast enough. At this rate, it would take many years for him to be rid of them. In the meantime, they provided a large pool of forced labor for jobs such as manufacturing uniforms and other clothing for the German army.

The following year, Hitler conquered most of Western Europe. He not only put the Jews living there under his control, he also regained control of thousands who—like Anne Frank and her family—had fled Germany during the 1930s. Serious restrictions were placed on their movements, and eventually they were forced to wear the yellow Star of David for quick identification.

Hitler turned on the Soviet Union, his former ally, in the early summer of 1941. The Wehrmacht, the German army, slashed deeply into Soviet territory. More than five million Jews in Lithuania, Latvia,

Heinrich Himmler was a primary organizer of concentration camps.

Himmler joined the Nazi Party after World War I, but left to become a chicken farmer. When he returned, he became one of Adolf Hitler's most trusted subordinates. He made numerous visits to the concentration camps during the war. He committed suicide before he could be brought to justice.

Estonia, the Ukraine, and Russia were added to the ones already under German control.

There was yet another "solution" for these unfortunate people. This was the *Einsatzgruppen,* or Special Action Groups. These groups had one task: to murder as many Jewish people as possible. Recruiting from among members of the SS, Himmler assembled about 3,000 men. These men—all volunteers who absorbed months of specialized training and anti-Jewish propaganda—were divided into four teams.

The *Einsatzgruppen* teams, following close behind the Wehrmacht, rounded up the Jews in each town with brutal efficiency. In many cases they were assisted by the town's non-Jewish inhabitants. Occasionally the captives would be gunned down near their homes. Far more often,

they were marched in large groups to open fields. Frequently they would be forced to strip naked. They would stand in long lines next to gaping ditches. *Einsatzgruppen* members would line up several yards away and kill them with bursts of rifle shots. The bodies would fall into the ditches. It was also common for the men to use their pistols at close range, shooting each person in the back of the head and quickly moving on to the next victim. Age and sex were no deterrents. Sometimes to save bullets, the men would rip infants from the arms of their mothers and club them to death with their guns. Then they would shoot the mothers.

When the killing had been completed, the bodies would be covered with chloride of lime so that they would decompose more rapidly. Then the ditches would be filled in with dirt. While the men of the

One of the German objectives was to take away the humanity of the Jews. Humiliating public searches were one method. When Jews arrived in the concentration camps, they would be given a number. None of the guards would refer to them by name.

Jewish people could be stopped for any reason and searched.

Einsatzgruppen were very efficient, sometimes a few people would remain alive as the dirt rained down on them. They would suffer the additional horror of being buried alive.

To the Nazi leadership, the work of the *Einsatzgruppen* was much better than slow starvation. Up to 20,000 people could be killed in a single day. According to some estimates, as many as 2.5 million people were killed in a few months.

But there were difficulties with this system. One was that some of the men in the *Einsatzgruppen* drank heavily and suffered nervous break-downs. Another was that too many people witnessed the killings. A third was that it couldn't be used in the West, where it would be more likely to come to the attention of the Allies.

The most notorious part of the Nazi plan for mass murder was about to begin.

By the end of 1940, an estimated half million Jews were packed into an area of about two square miles in Poland's capital of Warsaw. By contrast, the city's non-Jewish population of about one million had more than fifty square miles. Not surprisingly, starvation and disease claimed thousands of victims in the ghetto every month.

Somehow the people in the ghetto managed to worship, to read, even to dance and to laugh under the brutal conditions. Sometimes their total daily food intake consisted of a

A Nazi rounding up Jews

single serving of straw soup. But it became more and more difficult to survive, especially in mid-1942 when the Germans began sending them to the death camps. Over a period of about two months, some 300,000 people were removed from the ghetto. That reduced the population to about 60,000 and temporarily eased the burden on those who remained.

But they all knew what lay in store for them. They began assembling a pitifully small arsenal: a few rifles and pistols, a handful of precious machine guns, some primitive explosives. They also developed a complex system of tunnels to make it easier to move from one strongpoint to another.

In April 1943, the Germans decided to remove the ghetto's final inhabitants. To the soldiers' astonishment, the Jews fought back. Savage house-to-house combat continued for nearly a month. The brave men and women—whom the Germans called, "trash and subhumanity, cowards and bandits"—knew they could never win, but they believed it was important to resist. In the final days they even fought from the sewers.

Eventually the revolt was crushed. The German army had needed more than 3,000 soldiers, assisted by tanks and other armored vehicles, artillery, flamethrowers, and even airplanes to subdue them. The survivors were sent to the death camps, but the heroic fighters of the Warsaw ghetto had made history. They were the only organized group of Jews to openly resist Nazi oppression.

A concentration camp survivor dig
pile of cast-off clothing.

Two people for whom
rescue came too late lie
at the top of the picture.
During the war, corpses
were commonly stripped of
their clothing and anything
else useful. Some had gold
fillings in their teeth. The
teeth would be yanked out
and the gold melted down
and reused.

The Final Solution

In the fall of 1941, German army officer Adolf Eichmann opened a new department called the Race and Resettlement Office. On October 28, he wrote, "in view of the approaching final solution of the European Jewry problem" as he denied a petition by a Jewish woman who wanted to move from Germany to France.[1] This is perhaps the first time that the ominous phrase "final solution" appears in print.

Under Eichmann's plan, Jews all over occupied Europe were to be rounded up and taken to assembly points at major railheads. There they would be loaded into railroad cars and transported to several camps in Poland. They would be told that they were being "resettled."

The first of these "resettlement" camps was at the Polish village of Chelmno. On December 8, 1941, about 2,300 Jews were loaded in small groups into the backs of specially designed trucks. The trucks were sealed and the exhaust was piped into the back, killing all of them.

It didn't take long for the operation to shift into high gear. Three more camps were soon operational—Belzec, Sobibór, and Treblinka. Permanent gas chambers that could hold several hundred people at a time replaced the trucks.

On the morning of January 20, 1942, a number of senior Nazi bureaucrats met in the Berlin suburb of Wannsee. The meeting lasted less than ninety minutes. Members of the SS secured the cooperation of leading German officials in coordinating things such as railroad schedules. According to the minutes of the meeting, "In the course of this final solution of the European Jewish question, approximately 11 mil-

lion Jews may be taken into consideration."[2] There can be no doubt that everyone in attendance knew exactly what those words meant. The Nazis planned to kill every Jew in Europe.

The Nazis went to great lengths to keep the operation a secret. Many Jews themselves unknowingly helped. Most went willingly to the assembly points, clutching a few pitiful possessions to help them in their "relocation." The very enormity of the deed helped to keep it a secret. People found it hard to believe that such an evil thing could be done. Besides, they thought, why should the Nazis go to all the trouble of shipping them hundreds of miles away to kill them?

The deadliest of these camps, the one that claimed the largest number of victims, was Auschwitz. There were several reasons for its "success." Originally known by its Polish name of Óswiecim, it had a key location: almost exactly in the center of continental Europe. It was situated on a major railroad line. It was also miles away from any major population centers. It already had a number of World War I–era barracks.

The camp had been established in 1940, primarily to deal with political and Polish Army prisoners. In March 1942, a second camp was established near the neighboring village of Birkenau; it remained under the administrative control of Auschwitz. It was designed for Jewish prisoners alone.

Dozens of trains ran into Auschwitz every day. They passed through an archway, under the words *Arbeit Macht Frei* (work makes you free). The dazed Jews would climb out of the cars onto what became known as The Ramp. Most had spent days cooped up without food or water, often so tightly that there was no room even to sit. On arrival, some were already dead or dying. All the passengers were separated into two groups. Families were pulled apart.

The larger group—elderly, young children, mothers cradling infants in their arms—was told that they would take a cleansing shower, then rejoin their families. After having their heads shaved and neatly

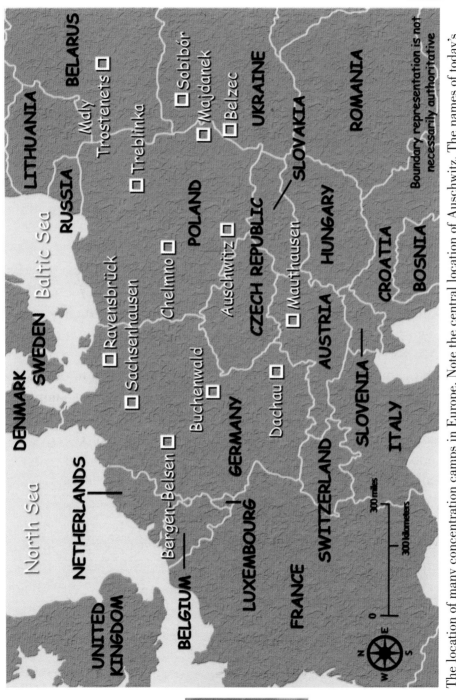

The location of many concentration camps in Europe. Note the central location of Auschwitz. The names of today's countries are shown in black lettering.

folding their clothing, they entered the "shower room" in groups of 200 or more. When the door was sealed shut behind them, a powerful insecticide called Zyklon B was dropped into the vents. Soon it began drifting into the room. Because it was heavier than air, the poisonous gas settled toward the floor. The panic-stricken victims would claw at each other, trying to rise higher to escape the fumes. It was hopeless.

When the screaming stopped, the doors would be opened. Prisoners called *sonderkommandos* (special detachments) would drag out the dead bodies. Before killing them, the gas would cause the victims to vomit and defecate, creating a mess and a terrible stench. The *sonderkommandos* not only had to clean up but also had to dig inside the mouth of every corpse, looking for teeth with gold fillings and extracting them. Melted down, the gold would provide still more luxuries for the Nazis. Then the *sonderkommandos* would load the bodies onto carts and take them to the ovens for burning. They sorted out the clothing, sending the best articles of apparel back to Germany. The clothing was accompanied by the victims' hair, which was used to stuff mattresses. Every so often, the *sonderkommandos* would themselves be gassed and new ones selected.

Some of the people who weren't immediately sent to the gas chambers were selected for "medical experiments" by the camp doctor, Josef Mengele. In one camp, he tied mothers to their beds immediately after they had given birth. That way they couldn't take care of their babies. His "research" had two objectives: to see how long it took for the children to die, and to see how long it took the mothers to go crazy.

The rest of the prisoners who survived the cruel first cut on the platform were stripped of their clothing and given the striped prison garments that have become gruesomely familiar to succeeding generations. A special pen and ink were used to tattoo a number into their forearms, and this information was entered on the prison rolls.

There was another purpose for the numbers. As writer Annette Wieviorka—whose friend survived Auschwitz—explains, "It stripped

them of their names, the last thing they had left. From then on they were called only by this number. They could never erase it. They had to repeat it in German every morning and night during roll call."[3]

Then a ceaseless round of misery began. The prisoners were jammed into crowded barracks. They generally were awakened before dawn and forced to stand for hours, often barefoot in thin garments, in freezing weather. Guards roamed up and down the line, punching prisoners at random. Falling could be fatal. Anyone who lingered on the ground was marked as a candidate for the gas chambers.

There was a reason for keeping them alive. Nearby coal deposits made Auschwitz a logical site for the establishment of heavy industry. It was also far enough from the German heartland to make attacks by Allied heavy bombers much less likely. These factories needed vast numbers of workers. Many of the prisoners were assigned to the chemical giant I. G. Farben, which manufactured Zyklon B. Others had the "good" jobs: working in the kitchen or in the warehouses, where plunder from dead prisoners accumulated. Some prisoners became musicians in camp bands; they played cheerful tunes to serenade those going off to work or to the gas chambers. A few worked for the prison administrators, helping them live "normal" lives.

As historian Doris Bergen notes, "Commandants and other high-ranking administrators often brought their wives and children to be near them. They had access to every luxury and of course to free labor. [Camp commandant Rudolf] Hoess's wife supposedly said about Auschwitz, 'Here I want to live until the end of my days.' Himmler authorized fish farms, gardens, and even zoos on the sites for the employees' benefit."[4]

There were no benefits for the prisoners. They lived in barracks with tightly packed "bunk beds," which were more like storage shelves. At least three or four people were squeezed onto each one. Since the barracks had no heat, the prisoners pressed their bodies together to provide a meager amount of warmth during the freezing nights. During the day, they would be employed as slave laborers, working up to twelve

hours without any breaks and receiving very little food. Since there was little running water and bathroom facilities were primitive, diseases were common. Deadly epidemics would sweep through the camp, claiming hundreds of victims whose immune systems had already been battered by the horrendous conditions.

The death toll at these camps would have been even higher if it hadn't been for the efforts of thousands of people, many of whom risked their lives to help the Jews before they were forced to board the fatal trains. Non-Jewish Danes helped nearly all the Jews in their country escape to neutral Sweden just ahead of Nazi efforts to deport them. German businessman Oskar Schindler not only saved more than 1,000 Jewish men who worked for him, but also managed to bring back 300 women who had been shipped to Auschwitz—the only known instance where people made a round trip in and out. A Japanese diplomat defied his government and gave safe-conduct visas to thousands of Jews. He lived in disgrace in Japan for the rest of his life. One of the most effective—and tragic—heroes was Raoul Wallenberg, a Swedish diplomat who saved up to 100,000 Hungarian Jews. He was captured by the Soviets early in 1945 and executed two years later.

In spite of all these efforts, the gas chambers continued their deadly work, and the crematoriums reduced human beings to ashes. But time was running out on the perpetrators of these horrible crimes.

There was another way of saving Jewish lives in addition to the heroic efforts made by people like Raoul Wallenberg and Oskar Schindler: killing Hitler. By 1943, a number of regular army officers became involved in a plot to assassinate him. They had a variety of motives. Some, especially those who were aristocrats, had always looked down on him because of his humble origins. Others were convinced that his often bungling efforts to dictate military strategy were bound to lead to defeat. Still others were appalled at the systematic murder of civilians. A few wanted to negotiate peace with the Western Allies, then team up with them and attack the Soviet Union. As the war continued, it seemed apparent to the officers that Hitler was going to destroy Germany.

Oskar Schindler

Gradually their plans took shape. A general staff officer named Claus von Stauffenberg had direct access to Hitler. He agreed to carry a bomb to a meeting at Hitler's forward headquarters, which was located east of Berlin. As soon as the bomb exploded, Stauffenberg would send word to other conspirators in Berlin. They would seize several key points in the capital and announce that they had taken control of the government.

On July 20, 1944, Stauffenberg took a briefcase containing the bomb into the meeting room. He slipped out, virtually unnoticed, a few minutes before it went off. From a safe vantage point, he watched and heard it explode. He was convinced that everyone in the room was dead. However, a heavy wooden panel between Hitler and the bomb had taken much of the force of the blast. Although several people were killed, Hitler was only injured. Coupled with the inability of the plotters to take advantage of a few hours when communications between Hitler and the capital were cut off, the plot failed.

Stauffenberg and hundreds of other plotters were executed. The war would continue for more than eight months and cost hundreds of thousands of additional lives.

U.S. soldiers cautiously advance in Julien, Germany, in February 1945

The last major German offensive, the Battle of the Bulge, had ended in defeat two months earlier. Yet the Germans continued to resist. They were especially stubborn in the east against approaching Soviet troops. Most of the capital city of Berlin was in ruins by the time Germany surrendered in May 1945.

Justice

One of the strange things about the Holocaust is that the Nazis diverted precious resources to the continuing murder of Jews even after it became apparent that the war was going against them. The Soviet victory at the Battle of Stalingrad in February 1943 marked the end of German expansion in the East. Gradually the Red Army forced the Germans back. In mid-1943, American and British troops landed in Italy. In June 1944, the D-Day invasion of Normandy, France, put hundreds of thousands of Allied troops ashore. Hitler's last gamble, the Battle of the Bulge at the end of the year, failed.

By early 1945, therefore, it seemed apparent that Germany was doomed. But the Nazis had a final horror for the people in the death camps. As Red Army soldiers drew closer, the guards forced most of the inmates to leave and marched them toward Germany. It is estimated that 60,000 inmates left Auschwitz. In bitter cold, many of them were barefoot, weakened by malnutrition, and wearing skimpy clothing. The "reward" for the few who managed to make the long trek was still more slave labor.

In March 1945, American and British troops crossed the Rhine River and entered Germany from the west. Hitler and a few of his closest, most fanatical followers retreated to an underground bunker in the heart of Berlin. Hitler committed suicide on April 30, a day after Joe Sacco had participated in the liberation of Dachau.

A week later, Germany surrendered.

As the news of Nazi atrocities spread around the world, many people demanded that the surviving German leaders be brought to

justice. Göring and other top Nazis were placed on trial as "war criminals" in Nuremberg. Nearly all were convicted.

Thousands of offenders escaped immediate punishment. Many were captured in the following months. Some melted away, helped by a network of former Nazis. When the Jewish state of Israel was established, one of its priorities was tracking down as many of these men as possible.

One of the most famous cases involved Adolf Eichmann, who had ordered millions of Jews to their deaths. He had vanished after the war. In 1959, Israeli Nazi hunters were tipped off. They found him in Argentina, living under an assumed name. They kidnapped him and took him to Israel for a trial that attracted worldwide attention. Eichmann's primary defense was that he was only following orders. His judges disagreed. He was convicted and hanged.

A few managed to escape justice altogether. Josef Mengele, the "Angel of Death" at Auschwitz, fled to Brazil. To the day of his death in 1979, he never expressed any remorse for his actions.

Nazi actions were one of the reasons that many of the survivors had no place to go. Their families and homes had been destroyed. Many foreign countries—including the United States—still maintained rigid quotas.

Many of the survivors wanted to go to Palestine, the original homeland of the Jews nearly 2,000 years earlier. The British would admit only a few. Thousands of others poured in despite the obstacles the British placed in their way.

Soon after its formation in 1945, members of the United Nations voted to establish a Jewish state in part of Palestine. The Arabs opposed it, and as soon as the British left in 1948 the Arabs launched an invasion. The Israelis fought back and defeated their numerically superior enemies. Even though the United Nations had also called for an Arab state to be established, it never happened. Over half a century and several wars later, the problem remains.

No one would ever say that the Jews were Hitler's only victims. Hundreds of thousands of prisoners of war, especially Poles and

Russians, were starved to death or murdered outright. So were the physically handicapped, the mentally retarded, homosexuals, Gypsies, communists, other political opponents, and many more. In fact, these crimes gave birth to our word *genocide,* which is the deliberate destruction of a group of people. But there was one important difference between the targeting of Jews and the targeting of other groups.

As history professor Robert Wistrich points out, "The Jewish Holocaust was unprecedented—as compared to other genocides—because it was the planned, deliberate policy decision of a powerful state that mobilized its resources to destroy the *entire* Jewish people."[1]

Many people believe that something as horrible as the Holocaust could never happen again. But the spirit that animated it is still alive. White supremacists and Nazi parties exist in Germany, the United States, and other countries. Men and women known as "skinheads" because they shave their scalps have tattoos that express admiration for Hitler and demand "white power." Jewish cemeteries are sometimes desecrated.

Martin Niemöller was a courageous Protestant pastor who managed to survive for seven years in the concentration camps. After his release, he made the following statement:

"In Germany they came first for the Communists, and I didn't speak up because I wasn't a Communist. Then they came for the Jews, and I didn't speak up because I wasn't a Jew. Then they came for the trade unionists, and I didn't speak up because I wasn't a trade unionist. Then they came for the Catholics, and I didn't speak up because I was a Protestant. Then they came for me, and by that time no one was left to speak up."[2]

Unfortunately, there will almost certainly always be people who are prejudiced against other people on the basis of religion, skin color, or other reasons. In the twenty-first century, this prejudice has led to the killing of large groups of people in Darfur (part of the Sudan) and Rwanda. Niemöller was saying that it is necessary to speak up against such acts, regardless of whether a person is part of the victimized group. That is the best way of preventing another Holocaust.

William Shirer

A few months after Germany surrendered, twenty-one captured Nazi leaders were placed on trial for war crimes in the city of Nuremberg. Its Palace of Justice was one of a few large buildings that hadn't been heavily damaged or destroyed by Allied bombing. Symbolically, the city had been important in the rise of the Nazis. It was the scene of the spectacular Nazi rallies in the 1920s and 1930s. It seemed appropriate that it should also be the scene of the party's final fall from power.

Journalist William Shirer, who had followed the rise of Hitler and many of the men on trial, noted: "Attired in rather shabby clothes, slumped in their seats fidgeting nervously, they no longer resembled the arrogant leaders of old."[3] One looked "like a contrite college boy who has been kicked out of school."[4] Grand Admiral Karl Dönitz, the architect of a U-boat campaign that nearly crippled the Allied effort to send supplies across the Atlantic Ocean, resembled "a shoe clerk."[5]

The proceedings were designed to provide fair trials for the accused men—something they rarely if ever gave the people who had been under their control for so many years. Each of the four major Allies—the United States, the Soviet Union, Great Britain, and France—had several prosecutors. The defendants selected their own lawyers. All but two pled "not guilty." They offered a defense that would become all too common: They were simply following orders.

The trials lasted for more than ten months. They concluded, ironically, on October 1—which that year fell on the Jewish religious holiday of Yom Kippur, the Day of Atonement. Three defendants were acquitted. Four were sentenced to prison terms of between ten and twenty years. Three more received life imprisonment. The other eleven were condemned to death. For them, justice was swift. In the early morning of October 16, 1946, they were hanged. There was one exception: Hermann Göring. Like Hitler and Himmler (who killed himself after being captured by the British), he chose to end his own life: He swallowed poison.

Chronology

1933	Adolf Hitler comes to power in Germany; Dachau, the first concentration camp, opens.
1934	Night of the Long Knives removes Ernst Röhm, Hitler's last political opponent.
1935	The Nuremberg Laws introduce official discrimination against Jews.
1936	Hitler orders German troops to occupy the Rhineland in defiance of the Versailles Treaty; Olympic Games attract many athletes and spectators to Berlin.
1937	In Germany, nearly every profession becomes closed to Jews.
1938	Austria becomes part of Germany; mobs rampage against Jews on Kristallnacht.
1939	Hitler begins World War II by invading Poland.
1940	Jewish ghettos in the Polish cities of Warsaw, Lodz, and Cracow are sealed off.
1941	The Einsatzgruppen begin activities in the Soviet Union.
1942	The Wannsee conference develops the Final Solution to the Jewish "question."
1943	Jews in the Warsaw ghetto rise up in a monthlong revolt.
1944	Allies land at Normandy; the plot to kill Hitler fizzles.
1945	The concentration camps are liberated; Hitler commits suicide; World War II ends; Nuremberg Trials begin.
1946	The Nuremberg Trials end.
1962	Adolf Eichmann is tried and executed.

Timeline in History

A.D. 67   Jews are forced to leave the Holy Land; they spread and settle throughout Europe.

962   The First Reich, also known as the Holy Roman Empire, begins; it lasts until 1806.

1096   In several cities, Christians in the First Crusade kill Jews en route to the Holy Land.

1144   Riots against Jews break out in Norwich, England, following charges that they ritually murdered a Christian child.

1348   Many Jews are killed after the outbreak of the Black Death, which they are blamed for causing.

1517   Martin Luther posts his 95 theses on the door of Wittenberg Castle Church, which begins the Protestant Reformation.

1543   Martin Luther publishes The Jews and Their Lies.

1871   The Second Reich (the German Empire) is established under Prussian leadership.

1881   A wave of anti-Jewish pogroms begins in Russia following the assassination of Czar Alexander II.

1889   Adolf Hitler is born in Austria on April 20.

1893   Hermann Göring is born in Rosenheim, Germany, on January 12.

1900   Heinrich Himmler is born in Munich, Germany, on October 7.

1914   World War I begins.

1918   World War I ends.

1936   Adolf Hitler uses the Olympic Games in Berlin as a showcase for his success in reviving Germany.

1941   The Japanese attack on Pearl Harbor, Hawaii, results in U.S. involvement in World War II.

1945   World War II ends; the United Nations is formed.

1948   The United Nations votes to create the Jewish state of Israel and a neighboring state for Arabs.

2005   Britain's Prince Harry faces severe criticism when he attends a costume party wearing a Nazi Party uniform.

Chapter Notes

Chapter One
Liberation
1. Jack Sacco, *Where the Birds Never Sing* (New York: HarperCollins, 2003), p. 276.
2. Ibid., p. 289.
3. Anne Frank, *The Diary of a Young Girl,* translated by Susan Massotty (New York: Doubleday, 1995), p. 336.

Chapter Two
The Nazis Take Over
1. "Medieval Anti-Jewism," http://www.aihgs.com/doc2.htm.
2. Professor Gerhard Rempel, "Hitler's Germany: A Study in Totalitarian Dictatorship." http://mars.acnet.wnec.edu/~grempel/courses/hitler/lectures/dictator.html.
3. William Shirer, *The Rise and Fall of the Third Reich* (London: Pan Books, 1960), p. 290.

Chapter Four
The Final Solution
1. Martin Gilbert, "The Final Solution." http://www.english.uiuc.edu/maps/holocaust/finalsolution.htm.
2. Ronnie S. Landau, *The Nazi Holocaust* (Chicago: Ivan R. Dee, Inc., 1994), p. 168.
3. Annette Wieviorka, *Auschwitz Explained to My Child,* translated by Leah Brumer (New York: Marlowe & Company, 2002), p. 5.
4. Doris L. Bergen, *War and Genocide: A Concise History of the Holocaust* (Lanham, Md.: Towman and Littlefield Publishers, Inc., 2003), p. 182.

Chapter Five
Justice
1. Robert Wistrich, *Hitler and the Holocaust* (New York: The Modern Library, 2001), p. 6.
2. "Martin Niemöller—Brief Biography and Bibliography" http://internet.ggu.edu/university_library/if/Niemoller.html.
3. William Shirer, *The Rise and Fall of the Third Reich* (London: Pan Books, 1960), p. 1355.
4. Ibid.
5. Ibid., p. 1356.

Further Reading

For Young Adults

Adler, David A. *A Hero and the Holocaust.* New York: Holiday House, 2002.

Brostoff, Anita (editor). *Flares of Memory: Stories of Childhood During the Holocaust.* New York: Oxford University Press, 1998.

Frank, Anne. *The Diary of a Young Girl.* Translated by Susan Massotty. New York: Doubleday, 1995.

Grant, R. G. *New Perspectives: The Holocaust.* Austin, Tex.: Raintree Steck-Vaughn, 1998.

Lawton, Clive. *Auschwitz: The Story of a Nazi Death Camp.* Cambridge, Mass.: Candlewick Press, 2002.

Levine, Karen. *Hana's Suitcase.* Morton Grove, Ill.: Albert Whitman & Company, 2003.

Rice, Earle Jr. *The Holocaust Library: The Final Solution.* San Diego, Calif.: Lucent Books, 1998.

Rogasky, Barbara. *Smoke and Ashes: The Story of the Holocaust.* New York: Holiday House, 2002.

Orlev, Uri. *Run, Boy, Run.* Translated by Hillel Halkin. New York: Houghton Mifflin, 2003.

Wieviorka, Annette. *Auschwitz Explained to My Child.* Translated by Leah Brumer. New York: Marlowe & Company, 2002.

Works Consulted

Bergen, Doris L. *War and Genocide: A Concise History of the Holocaust.* Lanham, Md.: Towman and Littlefield Publishers, Inc., 2003.

Landau, Ronnie S. *The Nazi Holocaust.* Chicago: Ivan R. Dee, Inc., 1994.

Rhodes, Richard. *Masters of Death: The SS Einsatzgruppen and the Invention of the Holocaust.* New York: Alfred A. Knopf, 2002.

Sacco, Jack. *Where the Birds Never Sing.* New York: HarperCollins, 2003.

Shirer, William. *The Rise and Fall of the Third Reich.* London: Pan Books, 1960.

Wiesel, Elie. *Reflections on the Holocaust.* Translated by Benjamin Moser. New York: Schocken Books, 2002.

Wistrich, Robert S. *Hitler and the Holocaust.* New York: The Modern Library, 2001.

On the Internet

Gilbert, Martin. "The Final Solution." http://www.english.uiuc.edu/maps/holocaust/finalsolution.htm

Martin Niemöller—Brief Biography and Bibliography http://internet.ggu.edu/university_library/if/Niemoller.html

Medieval Anti-Jewism http://www.aihgs.com/doc2.htm

The Other Reichs http://europeanhistory.about.com/cs/germany/a/Otherreichs.htm

Rempel, Gerhard. "Hitler's Germany: A Study in Totalitarian Dictatorship." http://mars.acnet.wnec.edu/~grempel/courses/hitler/lectures/dictator.html

Glossary

appeasement (uh-PEEZ-munt)
calming an enemy to avoid war, usually through giving up something of value.

contrite (kun-TRITE)
expressing regret for one's actions.

crematorium (kree-muh-TORE-ee-uhm)
a place containing ovens or furnaces for burning corpses to ashes.

emaciated (ih-MAY-she-ay-tid)
having become abnormally thin through starvation.

GIs (GEE-EYES)
American soldiers; stands for "government issue."

mesmerizing (mez-muh-RYE-zing)
exerting an almost hypnotic effect.

neutral (NOO-truhl)
not taking sides in a conflict.

oratory (OR-uh-tor-ee)
effective and eloquent public speaking.

pogrom (POE-grum)
the organized attacking and murdering of a particular group (most often Jews), often carried out with the encouragement of the government.

reparation (reh-puh-RAY-shun)
payment for wrongdoing, including damages done.

repudiate (rih-PYOO-dee-ate)
refuse to obey.

typhus (TIE-fuss)
a serious disease spread by fleas and lice, characterized by high fever, delirium, and rash.

Pronounciation Guide

Auschwitz (OUSH-vitz)
Belzec (BELL-zets)
Bergen-Belsen (BEAR-gun BELL-zen)
Buchenwald (BOO-kuhn-wald)
Chelmno (KELM-no)
Dachau (DAH-cow)
Majdanek (my-DAHN-eck)
Maly Trostenets (MAA-lee TROSH-teh-nets)
Mauthausen (MAWT-how-zen)
Ravensbrück (RAH-venz-brook)
Sachsenhausen (ZAHK-zen-how-zen)
Sobibór (SO-bih-bore)
Treblinka (TREH-blin-kuh)

Index

Anti-Semitism, roots of 13-15

Auschwitz 10, 11, 32, 34-36

Battle of the Bulge 38, 39

Belzec 10, 31

Bergen-Belsen 6, 10, 11

Berlin 10, 21

Birkenau 32

Buchenwald 10

Chamberlain, Neville 21

Chelmno 10, 31

Dachau 7-10, 20, 39

Darfur 41

D-Day 39

Dönitz, Karl 42

Dreyfus, Albert 15

Eichmann, Adolf 31, 40

Einsatzgruppen 26-28

Eisenhower, General Dwight 9

Enabling Law 19

"Final Solution," the 31-32

Frank, Anne 11, 25

Frank, Otto 11

German surrender 39

Gestapo 19

Ghettos 25, 29

Göring, Hermann 18, 19, 40, 42

Grynszpan, Herschel 21

Himmler, Heinrich 19, 20, 26, 42

Hindenberg, Paul von 19, 20

Hitler, Adolf 9, 10, 11, 12, 13, 22, 40, 41, 42

   Begins World War II 25

   Birth of 16

   Death of 39

   Establishes concentration camps 9–10, 20

   Occupies Rhineland 21

   and Olympics 23

   Plot to kill 37

   Rise to power 17–20

   Writes *Mein Kampf* 17

Hoess, Rudolf 35

Israel 40

Kahr, Gustav Ritter von 17

Kindertransport 22

Kristallnacht 21-22

Long, Luz 23

Luther, Martin 14, 15

Majdanek 10

Map 33

Marr, Wilhelm 15

Maly Trostenets 10

Mauthausen 10

Mengele, Josef 34, 40

Niemöller, Martin 41

Night of the Long Knives 20

Nuremberg 18, 20, 40, 42

Nuremberg Laws 20, 48

Owens, Jesse 23

Palestine 22, 40

Ravensbrück 10

Röhm, Ernst 19, 20

Rwanda 41

SA 19, 20, 24

Sacco, Joe 7–9

Sachsenhausen 10

Schindler, Oskar 36, 37

Shirer, William 42

Sobibór 10, 31

Sonderkommandos 34

SS 19, 20, 26, 31

Stauffenberg, Claus von 37

Treaty of Versailles 16, 17, 20

Treblinka 10, 31

United Nations 20, 40

Wallenberg, Raoul 36, 37

Wannsee Conference 31-32

Warsaw Ghetto Uprising 29

Zyklon B 34, 35